DATE DUE

MAR 2 0 2013	
JUN 2 9 2013	
MAR 1 2014	
JUL 1 9 2014	
SEP 2 0 2014	
NOV 7 2014	
DEC 1 0 2014	
DEC 2 2 2014	

MICHAEL DAHL **PRESENTS**

SUPER FUNNY

JOKE BOOKS

Chuckle
Squad

JOKES ABOUT
CLASSROOMS, SPORTS, FOOD, TEACHERS,
AND OTHER SCHOOL SUBJECTS

PICTURE WINDOW BOOKS
a capstone imprint

MICHAEL DAHL PRESENTS SUPER FUNNY JOKE BOOKS

are published by Picture Window Books
a Capstone Imprint
151 Good Counsel Drive, P.O. Box 669
Mankato, Minnesota 56002
www.capstonepub.com

School Buzz was previously published by Picture Window Books, copyright © 2003
School Daze and *Teacher Says* were previously published by Picture Window Books, copyright © 2004
Chalkboard Chuckles, *Goofballs!*, *Lunchbox Laughs*, and *School Kidders*
were previously published by Picture Window Books, copyright © 2005
Silly Sports was previously published by Picture Window Books, copyright © 2007

Library of Congress Cataloging-in-Publication data
is available on the Library of Congress website.
ISBN: 978-1-4048-5773-5 (library binding)
ISBN: 978-1-4048-6370-5 (paperback)

Art Director: KAY FRASER
Designer: EMILY HARRIS
Production Specialist: JANE KLENK

TABLE OF CONTENTS

SCHOOL KIDDERS:
School Jokes

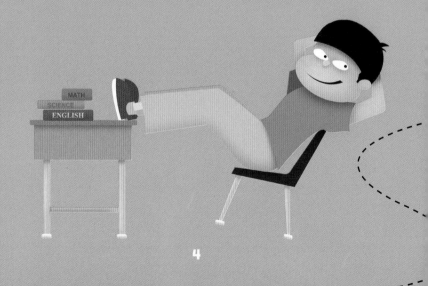

Who takes little monsters to school?

Their mummies.

Why was the broom late for school?

It overswept.

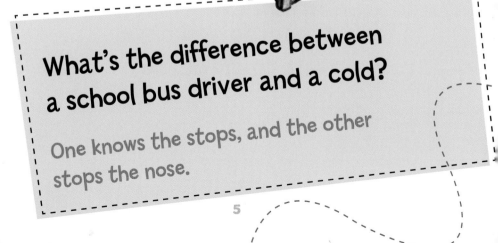

What's the difference between a school bus driver and a cold?

One knows the stops, and the other stops the nose.

What happened when the balloon got good grades?

It rose to the top of the class.

In what school do you have to drop out to graduate?

Sky-diving school.

What's the difference between a train and a teacher?

A train says, "Choo-choo," and a teacher says, "Spit out your gum!"

What kind of band doesn't make music?

A rubber band.

What do you call a student with a dictionary in his pocket?

Smarty pants.

What did the little turtles say to their teacher?

"You tortoise everything we know."

Teacher: Does anyone know which month has 28 days?

Student: All of them.

Why was the school clock punished?

It tocked too much during class.

Why do soccer players do well in school?

Because they really know how to use their heads.

What did the teacher do with the cheese's homework?

She grated it.

What flies around the school at night?

The alphabat.

What's the hardest thing about falling out of bed the first day of school?

The floor.

Why did the music teacher send the girl to the principal's office?

Because she was a treblemaker.

Which textbooks are the hardest to understand?

Math books because they have so many problems.

How did the music teacher unlock her secrets?

With piano keys.

Why did the computer have so many dents?

Because it was always crashing.

Why did the principal marry the janitor?

Because he swept her off her feet.

Why did the teacher send the clock to the principal's office?

Because it was taking too much time.

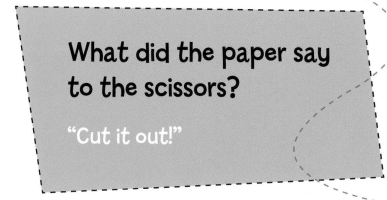

What did the paper say to the scissors?

"Cut it out!"

WHAT DID THE MAGNET SAY TO THE PAPER CLIP?

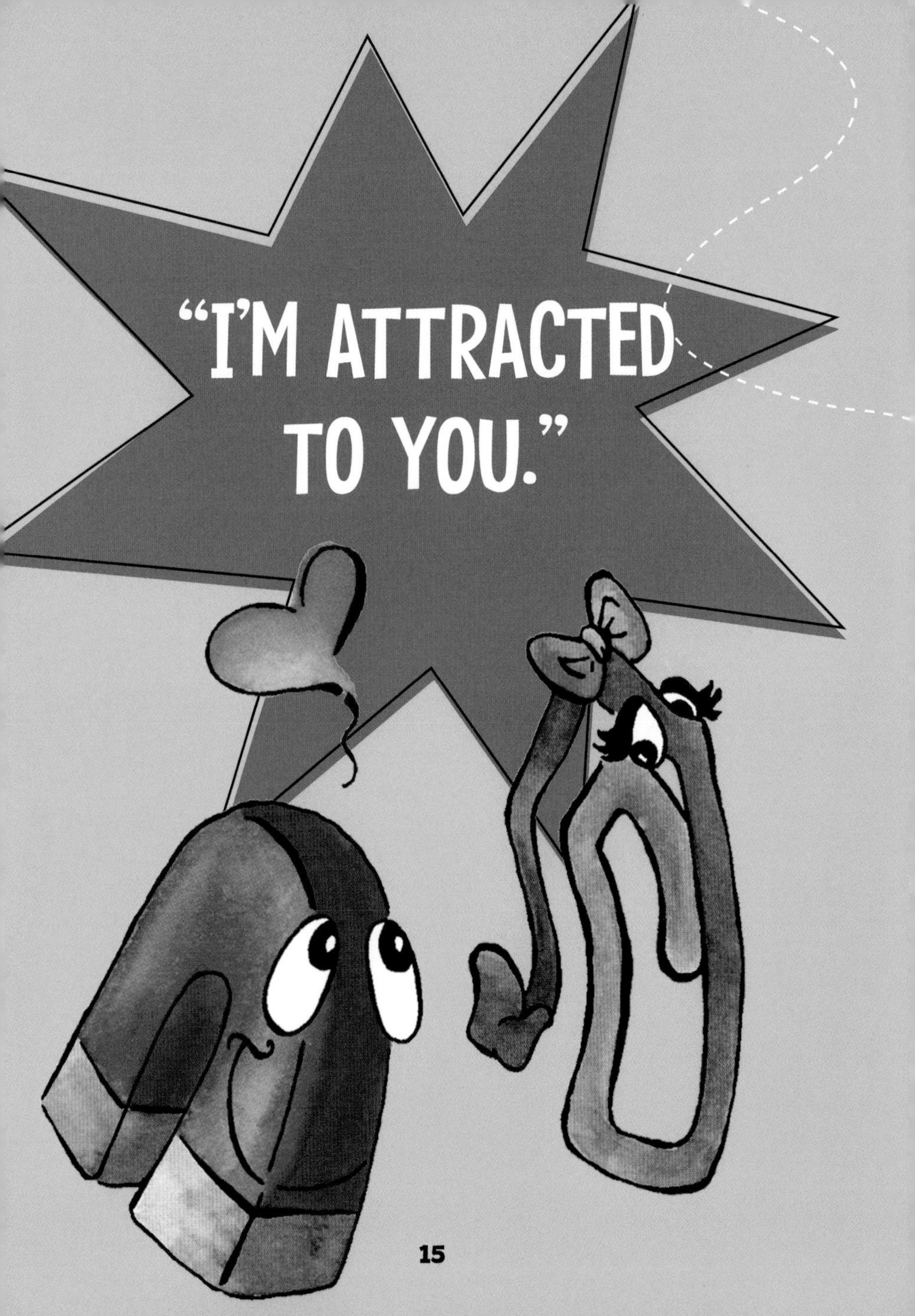
"I'M ATTRACTED
TO YOU."

What kind of shoes do lazy students wear?

Loafers.

Why did the kids give Johnny a dog bone?

Because he was the teacher's pet.

Why did the music student bring a ladder to class?

Because the teacher asked him to sing higher.

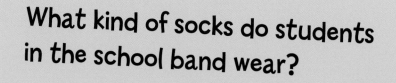

What kind of socks do students in the school band wear?

Tuba socks.

Where's the best place to learn how to make ice cream?

At sundae school.

Why did Jimmy do so well on the geometry test?

Because he knew all the angles.

What's black and white and read all over?

The pages of a textbook.

Why did the school cook bake bread?

Because he kneaded the dough.

Why is history always getting harder?

Because new things happen every day.

Teacher: I thought I sent you to the back of the line?

Student: You did, but someone else was already there.

What do music teachers give their students?

Sound advice.

Mom: **How do you like your astronomy class?**

Son: **It's looking up!**

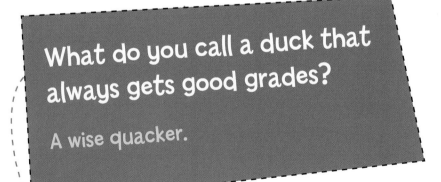

What do you call a duck that always gets good grades?

A wise quacker.

Teacher: **The answer to the math question is zero.**

Student: **All that work for nothing!**

Why was the school library so tall?

Because it had so many stories.

Why did the thermometer go to school?

It wanted to gain a degree.

Did the little tornado pass its math test?

Yeah. It was a breeze.

What did one math book say to the other math book?

"Boy do I have problems!"

Why did the student eat a dollar bill?

His mother told him it was for lunch.

What kind of fun do
math teachers have?

Sum fun.

Why did the girl bring a jump
rope to math class?

So she could skip the test.

WHY DID THE GIRL PUT ON LIPSTICK DURING CLASS?

THE TEACHER WAS GIVING A MAKE-UP EXAM.

Why did the boy eat his spelling test?

Because the teacher said it was a piece of cake.

Why did the student swallow all his pennies?

The teacher said he needed more sense.

Why did the girls wear swimsuits to school?

They rode in a car pool.

Why was the jungle cat thrown out of school?

Because he was a cheetah.

What was the snake's favorite class?

Hissssssssssssssssstory.

Why did the math teacher take a ruler to bed?

She wanted to see how long she slept.

What does a teacher get if he puts all of his students under a microscope?

A magnifying class.

How are elementary teachers like farmers?

They both help little things grow.

What was the witch's favorite subject in school?

Spelling.

Why did the nurse fail art class?

She could only draw blood.

Teacher: Why does the Statue of Liberty stand in New York Harbor?

Student: Because it can't sit down.

Who keeps track of all the meals in the school cafeteria?

The lunch counter.

30

What kind of pliers does a
math teacher use?

Multipliers.

What animal makes the best teacher?

A skunk because it makes the most scents.

What runs all
around the
school without
moving?

The fence.

Why did the student pour glue on her head?

To help things stick to her mind.

What kind of tree does a math teacher climb?

A geometry.

Teacher: Do you know the 20th president of the United States?

Student: No. We were never introduced.

Why is eight
afraid of nine?

Because nine ate seven.

Teacher: Why is the Mississippi such an unusual river?

Student: Because it has four eyes and still can't see.

Why was the math book so sad?

Because it had so many problems.

Teacher: Why are you reading the last pages of your history book first?

Student: I want to know how it ends.

How do bees get to school?

They take the school buzz.

Why did the student keep a flashlight in his lunch box?

It was a light lunch.

Parent: Would you like a pocket calculator for school?

Child: I already know how many pockets I have.

What kind of snack does the computer teacher like?

Microchips.

School nurse: Have your eyes ever been checked?

Student: No, they've always been blue.

What did the sloppy student get on his math test?

Peanut butter and jelly.

MATH

Where does the third grade come after the fourth grade?

In the dictionary.

What do you call a basketball player's pet chicken?

A personal fowl.

What has 40 feet and sings?

The school choir.

Science teacher: What is a light year?

Student: A year with very little homework.

Where does success come before work?

In the dictionary.

Why did the teacher wear sunglasses?

Because his class was so bright.

How did the new teacher keep his students on their toes?

He raised all of the chairs.

Why is six afraid of seven?

Because seven ate nine.

What did zero say to the number eight?

"Nice belt."

LUNCHBOX LAUGHS:
FOOD JOKES

Why did the cookie go to the doctor?

It was feeling crumby.

Why didn't the teddy bear eat dessert?

It was stuffed.

Why did the piecrust go to the dentist?

It needed a filling.

Why is corn such a friendly vegetable?

Because it's always willing to lend an ear.

What do ghosts eat for dessert?

Ice scream!

What food stays hot in the refrigerator?

Salsa.

What did the
farmer plant in
his sofa?

Couch potatoes.

Why don't eggs tell jokes?

They'd crack each other up.

How do you make a casserole?

Put it on roller skates.

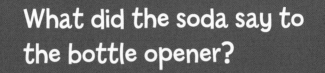

What did the soda say to the bottle opener?

"Can you help me find my pop?"

Why are strawberries such bad drivers?

They always get stuck in a jam.

Where do bakers
keep their dough?

In the bank.

Why did the waitress walk all
over the pizza?

Because the customer told her to
step on it.

What did the plate say to
the tablecloth?

"Lunch is on me."

What kind of lunch does a cheetah eat?

Fast food.

What did the hot dog say when it crossed the finish line?

"I'm the wiener!"

What did the astronaut put in his sandwich?

Launch meat.

Why did the orange lose the race?

It ran out of juice.

What do you use to fix a broken ketchup bottle?

Tomato paste.

What kind of fruit is never lonely?

Pears.

Why didn't the raisin go to the dance?

It couldn't find a date.

What do frogs eat with their hamburgers?

French flies.

Why did the little cookie cry?

His mother had been a wafer so long.

What vegetable do you get when an elephant walks through your garden?

Squash.

What do cheerleaders drink before a game?

Root beer!

Why did the doughnut maker sell his store?

He was tired of the hole business.

Why couldn't the monkey eat the banana?

Because the banana split.

Where do smart hot dogs end up?

On the honor roll.

What did the
gingerbread boy use
to make his bed?

Cookie sheets.

What is the worst kind
of cake to have?

A stomach cake.

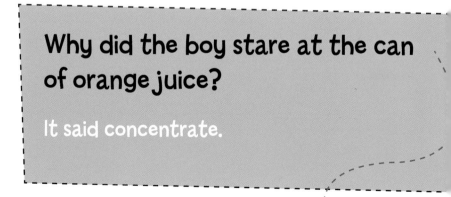

Why did the boy stare at the can
of orange juice?

It said concentrate.

How is a baseball team like a pancake?

They both need a good batter.

How do strawberries greet each other?

Strawberries shake.

What is the best thing to take before a meal?

A seat.

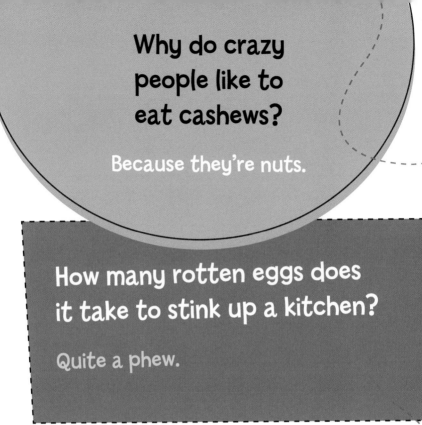

Why do crazy
people like to
eat cashews?

Because they're nuts.

How many rotten eggs does
it take to stink up a kitchen?

Quite a phew.

What kind of food is good for
your eyes?

Seafood.

Why did the banana
make so many friends?

Because he had a peel.

What do you get when you cross
a cow with a duck?

Milk and quackers.

Why did the sesame seeds get dizzy?

They were on a roll.

What did the hamburgers name their daughter?

Patty.

What do porcupines like to put on their hamburgers?

Sweet prickles.

What kind of shoes can you make from bananas?

Slippers.

GOOFBALLS:
SPORTS JOKES

What kind of hair do surfers have?

Wavy.

Why wouldn't they let the baby play basketball?

She wouldn't stop dribbling.

Why did Cinderella's team lose the volleyball game?

Because the coach was a pumpkin.

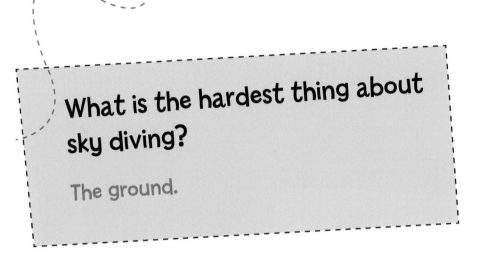

What is the hardest thing about sky diving?

The ground.

What color is a hockey score?

Goaled.

Why did the bowling pins refuse to stand up?

STRIKE

They were on strike.

Why did the golfer always wear two pairs of pants?

In case he got a hole in one.

Why is a soccer stadium the coolest place in the world?

Because it's full of fans.

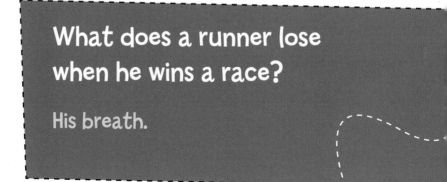

What does a runner lose when he wins a race?

His breath.

What is the quietest sport to play?

Bowling because you can hear a pin drop.

What is the loudest sport to play?

Tennis because players always raise a racket on the court.

What has 18 legs and catches flies?

A baseball team.

How can you tell that
elephants love swimming?

Because they never take their trunks off.

What's the difference between
a dog and a basketball player?

One drools and one dribbles.

Where do golfers go after a game?

To a tee party.

What do you call a girl who's good at catching fish?

Annette.

Why did the tennis player always carry a flashlight?

Because he lost all his matches.

What has wings and a skateboard?

Tony Hawk.

Why should you be careful playing sports in the jungle?

Because it's full of cheetahs.

Why did the frog try out for the baseball team?

He liked catching pop flies.

What do you call a pig
that knows karate?

A pork chop.

What is a
swimmer's
favorite game?

Pool.

Did you hear about the race between
the lettuce and the banana?

The lettuce was ahead.

Why do artists never win
when they play soccer?

The game always ends in a draw.

What football team travels with the most luggage?

The Packers.

Why did the chicken cross the basketball court?

It heard the referee calling fowls.

WHY DID THE SOCCER BALL QUIT THE TEAM?

IT WAS TIRED OF GETTING KICKED AROUND.

What is an electric eels favorite football team?

The Chargers.

Where can you find the largest diamond in the world?

On a baseball field.

What kind of insect is bad at football?

A fumble bee.

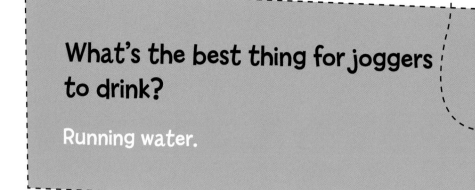

What's the best thing for joggers to drink?

Running water.

Why did the softball player take her bat to the library?

Her teacher told her to hit the books.

Why do the fastest bowlers make the most strikes?

They have no time to spare.

Why didn't the dog want to play soccer?

Because he was a boxer.

Why was Cinderella thrown off the school's soccer team?

Because she ran away from the ball.

Why did the jogger look so angry?

Because she was a cross-country runner.

How is a scrambled egg like a bad football team?

They both get beaten.

What did the right soccer shoe say to the left soccer shoe?

Between us, we're gonna have a ball!

Why shouldn't you tell a joke when you are ice skating?

The ice might crack up.

How do fireflies start a race?

Someone shouts, "Ready. Set. Glow!"

Why did the football coach send in his second string?

So he could tie up the game.

Why did the volleyball coach want the waitress to join the team?

He heard she was a good server.

Why can't you go fishing if your watch is broken?

You won't have the time.

What is a runner's favorite subject?

Jography.

What did the basketball player wear to the school dance?

A hoop skirt.

How are peaches and racetracks alike?

They both have pits.

What kind of cats like to go bowling?

Alley cats.

What is the best way to win a race?

Run faster than everybody else.

What did the baseketball say to the player?

You've really got me going through hoops for you.

What is the best advice to give a young baseball player?

If you don't succeed at first, try second base.

Why did the basketball player cancel his trip?

He didn't want to get caught traveling.

Why did the golfer bring a cage to the golf course?

She was hoping to get some birdies.

Why did the exterminator hire a bunch of outfielders?

He needed people who were good at catching flies.

What kind of tea do football players avoid?

Penalty.

What is the biggest team in the NFL?

The New York Giants.

HOW TO BE FUNNY

KNOCK, KNOCK!

The following tips will help you become rich, famous, and popular. Well, maybe not. However, they will help you tell a good joke.

WHAT TO DO:

- Know the joke.
- Allow suspense to build, but don't drag it out too long.
- Make the punch line clear.
- Be confident, use emotion, and smile.

WHAT NOT TO DO:

- Do not ask your friend over and over if they "get it."
- Do not speak in a different language than your audience.
- Do not tell the same joke every day.
- Do not keep saying, "This joke is so funny!"